The Cloud Princess

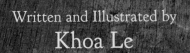

Written and Illustrated by
Khoa Le

INSIGHT KIDS

San Rafael, California

The Cloud Princess lived all alone
high up in the sky on her cloudy
white throne. She had no company
except for Miss Sun and Miss Moon.

"Dear Miss Sun, what is down there on Earth?" asked the curious Cloud Princess one day.

"There are so many things, sweetie," answered Miss Sun. "So many high buildings, so many green trees and colorful flowers. There are streets, towns, and cars that move very fast!"

"Children go to school every day.
They play games and share their toys.
There are animals: dogs, cats, chickens,
ducks, and many other birds."

The Cloud Princess wished that she could
see all those things with her own eyes.

One day in spring, the Cloud Princess decided
to travel closer to the Earth's surface.

Birds sang, flowers bloomed, butterflies and bees
flew all around her. She had never seen such
wonderful things, and it left her speechless.

"This is so beautiful!" she thought. "I have never seen anything like it before." The Cloud Princess was so excited by everything she saw that she flew lower and lower to the Earth below.

She was smelling a beautiful flower when suddenly she felt light-headed. It was a strange feeling, as though her whole body was melting.

She had begun to turn into
a million tiny water droplets.

"Hurry, dear, fly up!
Or else you are going
to become rain!"
shouted Miss Sun.

The Cloud Princess quickly flew back into the sky, but she was very sad that she had to leave the Earth behind.

Night and day, she sat on her cloud,
longing to see the world below again.

And so today, every now and then, the Cloud
Princess descends to the surface of the Earth and
takes a peek at the lovely scenery before flying
back up ever so quickly . . .

. . . bringing with her the spring rain.

KHOA LE is an illustrator, graphic designer, painter, and writer. She graduated from the Fine Arts University in Ho Chi Minh City. She has published thirteen books, seven of which she both wrote and illustrated. Her artwork has been featured in numerous exhibitions in Vietnam, Hong Kong, Singapore, and Korea.

INSIGHT
KIDS

PO Box 3088
San Rafael, CA 94912
www.insighteditions.com

 Find us on Facebook: www.facebook.com/InsightEditions
 Follow us on Twitter: @insighteditions

First published in the United States in 2016 by Insight Kids, an imprint of Insight Editions. Originally published in French in Switzerland in 2014 by NuiNui: © Snake SA 2014.

NuiNui ® is a registered trademark and registered by Snake SA.

Translation © Snake SA 2016
Chemin du Tsan Péri 10
3971 Chermignon
Switzerland

Library of Congress Cataloging-in-Publication Data available.

ISBN: 978-1-60887-731-7

ROOTS of PEACE   REPLANTED PAPER

Insight Editions, in association with Roots of Peace, will plant two trees for each tree used in the manufacturing of this book. Roots of Peace is an internationally renowned humanitarian organization dedicated to eradicating land mines worldwide and converting war-torn lands into productive farms and wildlife habitats. Roots of Peace will plant two million fruit and nut trees in Afghanistan and provide farmers there with the skills and support necessary for sustainable land use.

Manufactured in Shaoguan, China, by Insight Editions

20151201

10 9 8 7 6 5 4 3 2 1